The First Snow

M Christina Butler   Frank Endersby

LITTLE TIGER PRESS
London

Little Deer peeped out of his bed and blinked
in the morning sunshine.

"Yikes!" he squeaked. "Where's everything gone?"

Everywhere looked different. The wood was covered
with a huge white blanket.

Just then, Rabbit came skidding over, shouting, "Snow! Snow! Look at the snow!"

"Yippeee!" Squirrel cried, jumping out of a pine tree.

"What's happened?" squeaked Little Deer. "Where's all the grass gone?"

"It's under the snow," giggled Rabbit, beginning to dig. "Ta-daah!" he said as a tuft of icy grass appeared.

Little Deer nibbled a bit here and nibbled a bit there. The cold, crispy grass was very strange.

"Catch me if you can!" cried Rabbit, skipping off.

"Easy peasy," laughed Squirrel. "Come on, Little Deer!"

Little Deer stepped carefully into the cold, slippery snow . . .

BUMP!

He slipped and slid and landed on his bottom! He tried to get up again and . . .

BUMP!
THUMP!

He fell on his nose in a snowdrift!

"Ow-ooh!" he cried.
"I HATE the snow!
I want to go home!"

"Don't go, Little Deer," said Rabbit.
   "We're going to build a snowman!"
said Squirrel.
   "And we can't do it without you,"
added Rabbit.

So Rabbit made a snowball and
they all began to push.

Slowly it got bigger and bigger . . .

and soon it was so big they
couldn't push it any further!

"Let's make the snowman a head!" said Squirrel.
"He'll be bigger than me!" Little Deer laughed.
But with a creak and a groan the snowball began
to roll down the hillside.
"Oh no!" shouted Little Deer. "Stop that snowman!"

Slipping and sliding, they all chased down the hill. Faster and faster the snowball rolled, and faster and faster they tumbled after it . . .

SWOOSH! They skimmed off the bottom of the hillside, spun across the ice and landed, CRASH! in a big, snowy heap.

"That was awesome!" gasped Little Deer, as they all shook off the snow.

Slowly and slippily, wibbling and wobbling, they tried to stand up . . .

BUMP!

SWOOSH!

THUMP!

They skidded and slipped, and down they fell again and again! "Bother!" squeaked Squirrel. "Eeek!" giggled Rabbit.

"Hurray!" shouted Little Deer, up on his feet at last. "Let's skate!"

On and on they twirled until the moon shone bright, and stars twinkled in the deep blue sky. Little Deer's first snow had been such a surprise, but it had been the best fun ever!